Running

Marshall Cavendish
Benchmark
New York

This edition first published in 2010 in North America by Marshall Cavendish Benchmark

Marshall Cavendish Benchmark
99 White Plains Road
Tarrytown, NY 10591
www.marshallcavendish.us

Published in 2009 by Evans Publishing Ltd, 2A Portman Mansions, Chiltern St, London W1U 6NR

Editor: Nicola Edwards
Designer: D.R. Ink
All photographs by Wishlist except for page 6 © Michael Steele/Getty Images; page 9 © Gary M. Prior/Allsport UK/Getty Images; page 12 © Stu Forster/Getty Images; page 13 © Simon Bruty /Sports Illustrated/Getty Images; page 15 © Simon Bruty /Sports Illustrated/Getty Images; page 19 © Mark Dadswell/Getty Images; page 22 © Carl de Souza/AFP/Getty Images; page 23 © Adrian Dennis/AFP/Getty Images; page 26 © Oliver Morin/AFP/Getty Images; page 27 © Yuri Kadobnov/AFP/Getty Images

Library of Congress Cataloging-in-Publication Data

Gifford, Clive.
 Running/by Clive Gifford.
   p. cm. — (Tell me about sports)
 Includes index.
 Summary: "An introduction to running, including techniques, rules, and the training regimen of professional athletes in the sport"—Provided by publisher.
 ISBN 978-0-7614-4459-6
 1. Running—Juvenile literature. I. Title.
 GV943.25.G5492 2009
 796.334—dc22
                          2008049024

Marshall Cavendish Editor: Megan Comerford

Printed in China.
135642

The author and publisher would like to thank Logan Kelling, Amy Mobley, Tory Mobley, Aziz Olubaji, Connie McMillan, Liam Grieveson, Sharon Achia, and Ros Kelling (Coach) for their help in making this book.

Contents

Running

Dawn Harper of the United States in lane 6 crosses the line first to win a gold medal in the women's 100 m hurdles at the 2008 Olympic Games in Beijing, China.

People have held running races for thousands of years. At the very first Olympics, held over 2,700 years ago in Greece, there was only one event: a 190 meter (m) running race called a *stade*. This Greek word is the root of our word *stadium*.

Runners compete in races over different distances. The shortest events—the 60 m, 100 m, and 200 m—are known as sprints. Events such as the 800 m and 1500 m are called middle-distance races. The 5000 m and 10,000 m races and the marathon are long-distance events.

Today, millions of people run for exercise and fitness. Over 36,000 people, for instance, finished the 2008 New York Marathon. Some like to race against others, pushing themselves to run as fast as they can.

The very fastest runners in the world are record-breaking athletes. At the 2008 Olympics, Usain Bolt from Jamaica ran the 100 m in just 9.69 seconds, setting a new world record.

You may not break a world record, but you can record a **personal best (PB)**. This is when you run your fastest-ever time for a distance. Whether you win a race or not, beating your own best time should make you very proud. It's something that top professional athletes aim to do, too.

▼ Runners compete against others, but running is really a test of a person's own speed and ability.

Finishing First

Nothing beats the feeling of crossing the finishing line first in a race. Behind the glory of winning, though, there is a combination of skill and hard work.

▼ It is an amazing thrill to win a race and receive a trophy, medal, or certificate. It will inspire many athletes to train even harder.

▼ The runner in lane 4 is close to winning the race. She will thrust her chest forward as she runs through the finishing line.

To learn to run well, you need to work with a running coach or teacher. Coaches can give you exercises called drills to improve your fitness, speed, and running technique. That includes how you finish a race.

Toward the end of a race, you may start to feel tired. You might find it more of a struggle to run smoothly and, chances are, you will start to slow down. Top

▲ Gail Devers of the United States and Merlene Ottey of Jamaica finished with the exact same time at the 1993 World Championship 100 m final. Officials decided that Devers won the gold medal.

runners train very hard so they can fight this tiredness, which is known as fatigue. They try to stay relaxed and balanced throughout the whole race.

You must try to keep running as you cross the finishing line. This is because you only complete a race when your body crosses the line, not your arms or your legs. Young runners sometimes lose races if they do not time their finish well or slow down as they reach the line.

Really close finishes in major competitions are judged by high-speed photographs. These can separate out who has won even if two runners record exactly the same time.

Photo Finishes

At the 2007 World Championships, Lauryn Williams and Veronica Campbell finished the 100 m with the same time—11.01 seconds. Photo finishes showed that Campbell had won, but just barely!

At the 2002 European Championships, Mehdi Baala and Reyes Estevez ran the 1500 m race and crossed the line together. A photo finish showed Baala had won by just two thousandths of a second.

The Track

You will do most of your running on an athletic track. At school, this may be marked on grass. In stadiums, tracks are made of a special surface that provides grip. Outdoor tracks are 400 m long. Different races have different starting points. These are marked out on the track.

Tracks are usually marked with eight lanes. Lane 1 is the lane closest to the inside and lane 8 is the furthest away. Runners in the 100 m, 200 m, and 400 m have to stay in their lanes or they will be **disqualified**. This means they cannot take part in the race.

In longer races, runners may start in a lane but, after a certain distance, they can break. This means they can leave their lane. Runners usually move to the inside

▼ Runners in a 200 m race start from different places in their lanes. This is called a staggered start. It makes sure that all the runners run the same distance to the finish.

▲ Running fast around a bend in the 200 m can force you out of your lane if you are not balanced. The runner in lane 2 has stepped on the inside lane next to his. He will be disqualified.

lane because this is the shortest distance around the track.

When a runner completes the full length of the track, this is called a lap. In longer races, you may have to run many laps around the track. Runners try to stay on the inside of their lane.

When you are starting out you need a T-shirt, shorts, and good sneakers. Top track runners wear shoes with short spikes in the soles for grip. A tracksuit is also important because it will keep you warm between races.

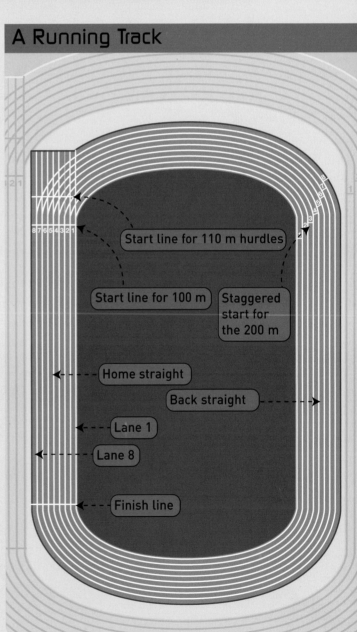

A Running Track

Start line for 110 m hurdles

Start line for 100 m

Staggered start for the 200 m

Home straight

Back straight

Lane 1

Lane 8

Finish line

Star Runners

▼ British hurdler Stu Jackson stretches his leg muscles before training. Stretching helps prevent injuries and helps your muscles perform well.

Top runners take part in races all over the world. The world's best runners become famous. Some become rich, too, since many competitions offer prize money to the winners and pay the runners a fee for appearing.

Runners spend hundreds of hours in training. They work very closely with their coaches and follow a strict diet. Runners not only have to be able to run fast. They

▲ Usain Bolt of Jamaica poses next to the Beijing Olympic stadium electronic
  timer that displays his 100 m world record of just 9.69 seconds.

also need strength. Sprinters especially need great power to surge forward at the start of their race.

Some professional runners have tried to cheat by taking drugs. Some drugs can improve athletic performance. Athletes can use them to build muscle quickly or train harder for longer periods. Athletes found guilty of taking drugs can be banned from entering competitions for two years or for life.

Amazing Athletes

As a child, Wilma Rudolph suffered from polio. She could only walk with leg braces. Yet she trained very hard, and in 1960 won the 100 m, 200 m, and 4 x 100 m relay races at the Olympics.

In 1968, Kenyan runner Kip Keino got caught in a traffic jam before his 1500 m race. He had to jog a mile (1.6 km) to the Olympic stadium, but he still won the gold medal for first place.

Josiah Thugwane was mugged and shot in South Africa. He recovered to win the marathon at the 1996 Olympics just five months later.

Sprints

Sprints are probably the most exciting running events. Millions tune in to watch male and female sprinters compete in the thrilling 60 m, 100 m, and 200 m races.

A sprint begins with the starter calling, "On your marks." You place your hands just behind the starting line.

▲ Adult sprinters use starting blocks to begin their races. These are metal bars with large wedges fitted to them.

On the call of "Set," you raise your hips up and press your feet hard against the track, ready to race.

▼ At the start of a sprint race, you should be in a low position during your first few steps. Then you need to straighten and run upright.

When the starter fires a gun or shouts, "Go!" you push off the track to get started. You bring your back leg forward to take your first step, called a stride.

You need to start as fast as possible, but you should try to avoid making a **false start**. When this occurs, officials judge you to have left your starting block before the starter's gun.

According to new rules in professional athletics, after one false start, the next person to make a false start will be disqualified. Electronic sensors fitted to the starting blocks determine if a sprinter has made a false start.

▼ This photo shows the men's 200 m final at the 2008 Olympics. Sprinters run with a good rhythm and look straight ahead. They pump their arms back and forth to help maintain their speed.

Middle-distance Running

The main middle-distance events are the 800 m and 1500 m. In the 800 m, runners start in lanes just as in sprint races. After the first bend (about 100 meters), they can break and head toward the inside lane. In the 1500 m, runners start along the same line and can move immediately to the inside lane if they want to.

▼ Runners stand up and lean forward for the start of a 1500 m race. They wait for the starter's gun to begin the race.

When you compete in a middle-distance race, it is usually impossible to run at full speed for the whole distance. Some runners get excited and run too fast at the start. This leaves them too tired to compete at the finish. It's important to judge carefully how fast you run during the different stages of a middle-distance race.

Try to run smoothly with your body upright and your shoulders level. Your arms should swing back and forth, but not as fiercely as when you are sprinting.

A bell rings to signal the last lap of a middle- (and long-) distance race. Then the pressure builds as runners try to get to the front or into position to challenge the leader. As you come around the final bend you may be tired, but you must try to sprint as hard as you can to reach the finish.

▼ To run middle-distance races well, try to run on the balls of your feet with a bouncy stride. As you push off your back leg, it should straighten behind you.

Hurdling

The base points toward runners.

▲ Hurdles have to be the correct height for your age. Your coach will adjust the hurdles to the right height for you.

▼ You push off your back leg and lift your front knee high. Straighten your front leg to get it over the hurdle. Pull up your back leg and turn your foot outward. Bring your back leg around to the front to land on the track.

Hurdling races are a great test of speed and skill. Top hurdlers complete 100 m and 400 m races in only a few seconds more than runners who are racing the same distance without hurdles.

There are ten hurdles to clear in the women's 100 m and men's 110 m. Each hurdle has a base, which means that it will fall over if a runner hits it during a race. Runners are allowed to knock over hurdles, but doing that slows them down and could make them fall.

The base of the hurdle always points toward the runner. Never try to jump a hurdle from the wrong side. You could hurt yourself badly if you do.

Good hurdling technique requires lots of practice. You raise and straighten your front leg and tuck your back leg to the side in order to clear a hurdle.

Top hurdlers need to be very flexible. They do a lot of stretching exercises. They also work with their coaches on their **stride pattern**. This is the number of steps they take in between hurdles.

Top Hurdlers

American Ed Moses set a record when he won 122 400 m hurdle races in a row between 1977 and 1987.

Liu Xiang won the 110 m hurdles at the 2004 Olympics. It was China's first gold medal for running. Two years later Xiang broke the world record with a time of 12.88 seconds.

▼ China's Liu Xiang leads at the 2004 Olympics 110 m hurdles final. A top-level hurdles race is an amazing sight. The hurdlers barely alter their running style as they sprint down the lanes and leap over hurdles.

Relay Racing

Relay races may be fun events at school, but they are very important in professional athletics. The relay events are often the final races at major competitions like the Olympics.

There are two main relay races in major athletics. Both feature four runners who all run the same distance. In the 4 x 400 m, each runner completes one lap of the track. A hollow tube called a **baton** is passed from one runner to the next.

The 4 x 100 m is the most dramatic relay event. You sprint as hard as you can to complete your 100 m of the

▼ The baton can be swept up or swept down into the receiver's hand. When receivers feel the baton in their hand, they grip it and sprint away.

Relay Records 🏃🏃🏃🏃🏃

Men
4 x 100 m 37.10 sec.
    —Jamaica, 2008
4 x 400 m 2 min., 54.29 sec.
    —United States, 1993

Women
4 x 100 m 41.37 sec.
    —East Germany, 1985
4 x 400 m 3 min., 15.17 sec.
    —USSR, 1988

▲ The receiver starts sprinting a few yards before the start of the changeover zone.

Start of the changeover zone

Dropped baton

▲ Relay runners need to communicate well. You can lose time with a slow baton pass or if you drop a baton.

End of the changeover zone

▲ If a runner steps out of the changeover zone before the baton is in the receiver's hand, the whole team is disqualified.

race with the baton in one hand. As you near your teammate, he or she starts to sprint.

You need to time the passing of the baton well. It must take place within a 20-meter stretch, which is marked on the track. This is called the **changeover zone**. Relay runners practice the baton pass a lot so they won't make a mistake in the race.

Relay teams think hard about the order in which they will all run. Often, a team will put its fastest runner in the last leg of a relay. But all runners must do their best if the team is to have a chance of winning.

Long-distance Running

▲ Male athletes run the 2008 Olympic marathon. Kenya's Samuel Kamau Wansiru won in 2 hours, 6 minutes, and 32 seconds, setting a new Olympic record.

Long-distance races are run over distances of 3000 m right up to the 26.2-mile-long (42.2 km) marathon. Top long-distance runners need good speed and strength. They also need stamina. This is the ability to run well for long periods of time.

Most long-distance races are run on normal 400 m tracks. In the case of the 10,000 m, that's 25 laps! Top runners such as Ethiopia's Haile Gebrselassie can still sprint the last 100 to 200 m of a race. The other main events run on a regular track are the 5000 m and 3000 m.

The 3000 m steeplechase is an unusual event. Runners have to jump or hurdle twenty-eight large barriers in a race. They also have to clear seven water jumps.

Some long-distance races are run on cross-country courses. Runners go through woods, up hills, and down into valleys. Other events, such as the marathon, are held on courses through city streets.

The marathon is the ultimate long-distance running test. Top athletes complete the course in less than two and a quarter hours. A marathon usually ends with a single lap on an athletic track.

Marathon Magic

The world's fastest marathon was run in 2 hours, 3 minutes, and 59 seconds by Haile Gebrselassie in 2008. The great Ethiopian was also undefeated in the 10,000 m from 1993 to 2001!

Another Ethiopian, Abebe Bikila, won the 1960 Olympic marathon. He ran the race in bare feet.

The Czech long-distance runner Emil Zatopek won the 5000 m, the 10,000 m, and the marathon at the 1952 Olympics.

▼ Runners in a steeplechase have the choice of hurdling obstacles or, if they are tired, they can put their foot on the top of the barrier and jump from it.

Running Tactics

▲ Long- and middle-distance running is tiring, especially if you are running front. Sometimes a group of runners will break away from the pack. The athletes in the group may take turns running at the front. They aim to keep lots of distance between them and the runners behind them.

▲ When you are running a middle-distance race, stay aware of your position among the other runners. You do not want to be boxed in with only a short distance of the race still to go.

Most runners aim to run at a fast, even speed for all, or nearly all, of a race. With longer races, it is possible to change how you race. Trying different ways of racing is called using tactics. Runners change their tactics based on their own strengths and weaknesses. They also have to think about the conditions (for example, whether it is raining or windy) and the other competitors in the race.

Some runners prefer to go faster at the start to get ahead and then try to stretch their lead. This is called running from the front and it can be very hard and tiring.

Other runners choose to run at a moderate pace and stay with the middle **pack** of runners. Near the end of the race, they increase their speed and hope to sprint past their rivals. In a close race when all the runners are bunched together, athletes have to be careful. They must avoid becoming boxed in, or trapped, by other runners. Otherwise they cannot get near the front.

Tactics can change from one race to the next. At top competitions, many runners have to take part in races called **heats**. The best runners from these races go into the semifinals or the final race. Some runners choose to slow down to save energy for a later race. Others prefer to run as fast as possible and record a time that makes their rivals nervous.

Drastic Tactics

Before digital watches, Paavo Nurmi of Finland raced with a stopwatch in his hand. It did not stop him winning an amazing nine Olympic gold medals!

Kenyan John Kagwe had to stop twice to tie his shoelaces during the 1997 New York City Marathon. He still won!

▼ If you have a sprint finish, you need to time it well. The runner on the left has been running behind the leader. When he is ready, he will move to the side of the leader and then run past him.

The World of Running

Running races range from competitions between local schools right up to international championships. Most countries have their own national athletics competition. These events can be important since the best runners may qualify to represent their country at a major international competition.

▼ American 400 m star Jeremy Wariner (holding the baton) leads the 4 x 400 m relay at the 2008 Olympics.

In the winter, indoor track competitions are popular. For many top runners, indoor racing helps them prepare for the outdoor season in the spring and summer. Indoor races take place on a 200 m track. The 100 m sprint is replaced by a 60 m sprint and the 100 m and 110 m hurdles are replaced by the 60 m hurdles.

Outdoors, runners compete in major events held in Europe and at championships such as the Pan-American games. The biggest competitions include the World Athletics Championships, which is now held every two years.

The Summer Olympics is the biggest competition of all. Held every four years, top runners dedicate much of their lives to try and win an Olympic gold medal. Millions of people tune in to watch the top runners compete in the Olympics.

▶
Maria Mutola of Mozambique wins her 800 m race at the 2006 World Indoor Championships.

Record Wins

At the 1948 Olympics, Fanny Blankers-Koen from The Netherlands set a record by winning four gold medals at the same games.

Usain Bolt won the 100 m and 200 m at the 2008 Olympics, breaking the world record time for each event.

Where Next?

These websites and books will help you to find out more about running.

Websites
http://www.iaaf.org
Read news and see action from important meetings at the website of the International Association of Athletic Federations, the organization that runs world athletics.

http://www.justrun.org
There's lots of advice on diet, training, and running tips at this useful website.

http://www.kidsrunning.com/
Produced by *Runner's World*, this is one of the best running websites for children.

http://www.olympic.org/uk
Learn about all the running events at the Olympics, including past champions from Athens in 1896 to Beijing in 2008.

Books
Goodrow, Carol. *Kids Running: Have Fun, Get Faster, and Go Further*. Halcotsville, NY: Breakaway Books, 2008.

Bodden, Valerie. *Running* (Active Sports). Mankato, MN: Creative Education, 2009.

Running Words

baton The short tube passed between relay runners in a race.

changeover zone A 20-meter area of the track where the baton is passed between runners in a relay race.

disqualified Barred from competing in an event for having broken a rule of the race.

false start An error made by an athlete when he or she starts running forward before the start of the race.

heat An early race in an event with the best runners advancing to a final or semifinal.

pack The main group of runners in a middle- and long-distance race.

personal best (PB) A runner's best-ever time for a particular event.

stride pattern The number of steps a hurdler takes between hurdles.

Index

Numbers in **bold** refer to pictures.